Remembering
Grandad

FACING UP To Death

Gianni Padoan   Illustrated by Emanuela Collini

Published by Child's Play (International) Ltd
Swindon   **Bologna**   **New York**
© 1987 Happy Books Milan Italy   ISBN 0-85953-311-5   Printed in Singapore
English Language Edition © Child's Play (International) Limited
This impression 1992   Library of Congress Catalogue Number 90-48380

FACING UP SERIES

Other titles

Break-up

Danger Kid

Follow my Leader

It was Thursday morning, and we were in the Sports Hall.
"Right!" said Mr Hughes. "As soon as your name is called you can start warming up over the jumps."
"Psst! Joe!" I whispered. "Where's James?"
"Gwen!" said Mr Hughes. "Be quiet, please!"
"Sorry, Sir. I wondered where James was."
"We had a phone call from his parents," explained Mr Hughes. "His grandfather is very ill."

After school, Joe and I walked home.
"I hope his Grandad's all right," Joe said.
"Me too," I agreed.
"He's like a second Dad to James. Did you know that James lived with his grandparents for a whole year?"
Joe nodded. "It was when his Mum and Dad were in Hong Kong, wasn't it?"
"Let's go and see James," I suggested. "We can find out how his Grandad is."

When we got to James's house, no-one was there. Everything was locked up. "Where is everybody?" Joe wondered. "Perhaps they're all round at the hospital, taking his Grandad flowers and grapes."
"Let's ask Mrs New next door," Joe suggested. "She knows everything that goes on in this street."

Mrs New looked as though she had
been expecting us.
"It was two o'clock in the
morning," she said. "They got a
phone call that James's Grandad was
very ill. They went to the hospital.
Victoria ward, I think."
"How is he now?" I asked. "Is he
better?"
"I don't know," replied Mrs New.
"I haven't seen anyone today. They
may still be at the hospital. Or
they may be staying with James's
Grandma."

We thanked Mrs New, and walked down the street.
"Shall we ring the hospital?" suggested Joe.
"Let's try his grandparents' house first," I replied.

To our surprise, James himself answered the phone.
"My Grandad's much better. He's coming home at the weekend, and we will be able to go cherry-picking after all!"

The sad ending came a week later.
Joe's Mum told him as soon as he
walked in the front door, after
school.
"I've got some bad news," she said.
"James's parents have just phoned.
His Grandad suddenly became ill
again. They rushed him to the
hospital, but this time he didn't
recover."

It was the same story at my house.
"It's not fair!" I said to Dad when
he told me. "He can't die now. He
has only just got better. They
went cherry-picking on Sunday!"
"I know, love," said Dad. "They
were very special friends, weren't
they? James will miss his Grandad.
But perhaps it's for the best. At
least the old man wasn't in any pain."

"Why don't you and Joe go and visit
James?" said Mum. "Dad will give
you a lift."

We called for Joe, and he came out of the house carrying a red parcel. "I baked James some of my special cakes," he said. "That should cheer him up."

As soon as we arrived, I dashed out of the car and gave James a special hug. Joe did too. I think he was pleased to see us.
Dad was talking to James's parents, so the three of us went into the kitchen.

I gave James the cakes, but none of us felt like eating. Nobody knew what to say. Finally, Joe broke the silence.

"You must be sad," he said. "I was sad when Rover died."

"It's not the same," I said. "Pets are different!"

"I really loved Rover," said Joe. "But I hardly remember my Grandpa. I got a pair of binoculars when he died."

"I was little when my Grandad died," I said. "But I will always remember playing on his knee."

"Do you remember when one of Milly's kittens died?" James said. "I ran and told Grandad. 'Why doesn't Milly care?' I asked. 'She's feeding the others as if nothing had happened.' Grandad thought for a moment. 'Maybe she does care, James. It's always sad when creatures die before their time, especially for their parents.

'But Milly has to take care of the others, or *they* would die. Death is part of living, and we can't spend all our lives worrying about it.' 'When someone dies, it's sad for the people who miss them. Grandma will miss me when I die. Sometimes people are sad because they've been mean and can't say sorry any more. But you don't need to be sad for the person who dies.'

'I'd miss you,' I said. 'I'd be lonely if you weren't here.'

'There's no need for you to be sad for me,' said Grandad. 'I'm old and I've had a full life. But I hope you'll think of me sometimes and remember cherry-picking, fishing in the river and you falling in. Now, put this hat on, and let's play pirates!'
'Oh, no you don't!' Grandma said as she came into the room. 'Time for your medicine and a rest!'"

The funeral took place a couple of days later. We met James at his Grandma's house. Nearly everyone in the village turned up to join the procession.
"I wonder how many people will be at *your* funeral?" I whispered to Joe. He thought for a moment. "Not as many as this," he replied. "There were only nine at my last birthday party."
I looked at the people. They didn't seem sad. James's Grandma had been crying, but she was smiling as she talked to the guests.
James's parents looked tired. As for James himself, he wasn't smiling, but he wasn't upset, either.

There was a short service. People said nice things about James's Grandad.
"I don't like this," whispered Joe. "I don't want my body to be burned."
"It's what Grandad wanted," replied James. "He said that his body would only be an empty shell."

James was quiet and far away in the days after the funeral. He told me and Joe later that he was worried in case he forgot his Grandad. So he spent as much time as possible thinking about him. He tried to think about Grandad in an everyday sort of way. What would he have done here, what would he have said there.

He even imagined his Grandad was around to help him with his lessons.

As the days went by, James became more and more like his old self. We went for a picnic one day with James's parents. James brought his Grandad's old fishing rod. "You've got to find a still pool in the river if you want to catch a trout," he said. "That's what Grandad told me." And he sat down and waited.

Joe and I were exploring the woods when we heard James shouting. We ran back, and there was James reeling in this huge fish. "Look at this!" he was shouting. "Grandad was right!"

I asked James the other day whether he was ever sad about his grandfather dying. He shook his head.

"Not really," he said. "And I don't miss him like I did at first. You see, when I go to my room, there's a photo of us on my desk, and a whole album of the times we spent together. His fishing rod is in one corner, and the kite we built is hanging on the wall. Grandma gave me the notebook with the drawings of trees and leaves in it. I've got his collections of feathers and pine cones and shells. And I've got his favourite story books."

"Last night," James went on, "I sat and looked at the stars from my window. I tested myself on their names, and I think I know as many as Grandad, now. Yesterday afternoon, I flew my kite in the fields at the back of Grandma's house, and I imagined Grandad running out to meet me. All these things remind me of him. All the sadness is gone. Remembering Grandad makes me happy."